About the Author

Mathieu Cailler is an award-winning author of fiction, poetry, and children's books. For more information, please visit www.mathieucailler.com.

Hi, I'm Night

Mathieu Cailler
Illustrations by Carrie Louise and Rebecca Wood

Hi, I'm Night

Olympia Publishers
London

www.olympiapublishers.com
OLYMPIA PAPERBACK EDITION

A CIP catalogue record for this title is
available from the British Library.

ISBN: 978-1-78830-692-8

First Published in 2020

Olympia Publishers
Tallis House
2 Tallis Street
London
EC4Y 0AB

Printed in Great Britain

Dedication

For Neebs, Big Al, and Sweet Lou

Dearest Children,

Hi, I'm Night.

This is the first time I've ever been able to address you. The reason I write you is because I'm very sad. Recently, I found out from my twin sister, Day, that some of you are afraid of me – scared of the dark.

To be honest, it made me cry.

You see, Day and I were born this way, long ago, in control of time and light. We have taken shifts for centuries to make sure you – and the rest of the world – is happy and taken care of. Day and I see each other twice during each 24-hour cycle, once at sunrise and once at sunset, when it's not really light or dark, but a combination of both.

I, my children, am nothing to fear. I'm here to give Day a break, and she is here to give me a rest. It's nice this way, the two of us, working as a team.

Day and I had a mom and a dad. They were stars. And this was just the way it was for us. It was our destiny.

You'll have a destiny, too. Something you'll be good at.

At first, Day and I didn't know how to apply our gifts. We took turns with darkness and light every hour. But after a couple of months, we learned that the world worked best when it was day for a while, then night for some time. This even split allowed the trees, the soil, the animals, the sea, and, most importantly, you to be productive.

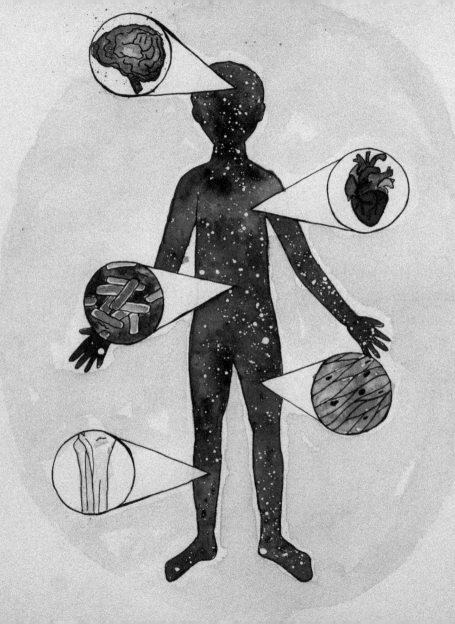

My darkness allows you to grow, helps your heart to relax, keeps your muscles healthy, aids in fighting infection, and makes you sharp and smart for when Day takes over. Plus, my darkness allows my stars to sparkle.

They're nice, right?

It's the same sky, children, just a different color.

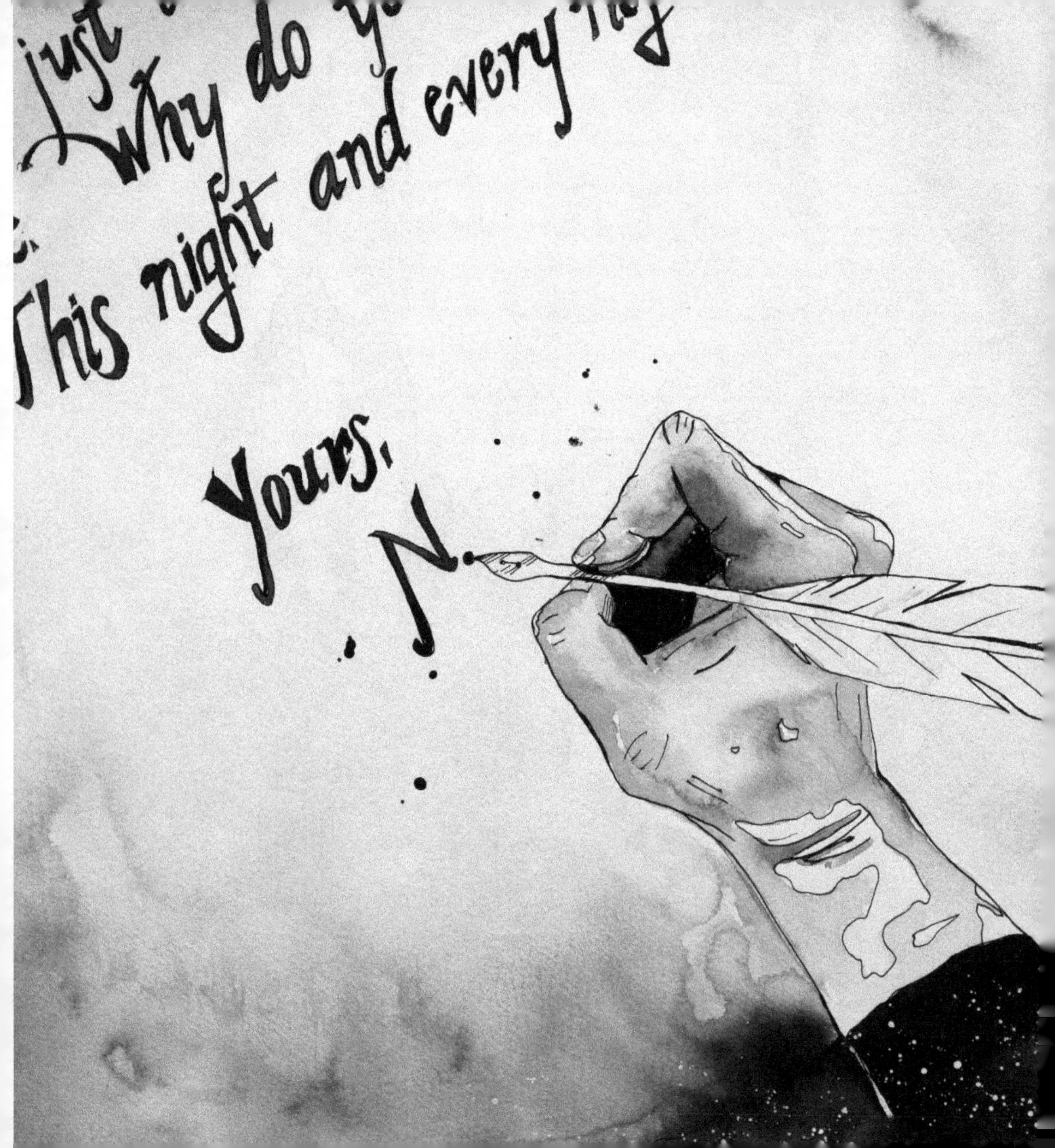

just
Why do
This night and every
Yours,
N.

I'm good for you. I promise. Why do you think people say "goodnight"? I bid you a beautiful sleep, dearest child. This night and every night.

Yours,

N.

CPSIA information can be obtained
at www.ICGtesting.com
Printed in the USA
LVHW061432071220
673543LV00029B/500

9 781788 306928